The Rules to the Street Game That Every Hustler Should Know!

"AM I MY BROTHER'S KEEPER?"

"The Realest Game expressed from a ghetto perspective".............

Written by:

G-prince

http: www.Ghettotheory.com.
Email Address: ghettotheorywriting@yahoo.com

Copyrights 2012
ISBN_978-0-9897486-4-3

Introduction

This book is written and dedicated to all of the young hustlers, gangsta's, and players who choose to participate in the ghetto game. Because what you don't know can surely kill you, therefore, it's about time to set the rules straight! "For it's a lot of you hustlers out there in the world, who's caught-up in the street game, but got the rules missing".

Your father, uncles, or big brothers never had a chance to properly lace you in the game, so you guys are out there getting caught-up on stupid shit that is costing you your life. And a lot of you hustlers do have a lot of game and knowledge about yourself, but it's the things that you don't know or shall I say, that you've never been properly exposed to, is getting you caught-up. And it's only right that I take the initiative to try to give you this wisdom and lace you in the *Real Rules* of life, which will broaden your understanding of the street game, and help you to better understand the consequences, pain, and scandalous deception that do exist out there.

Hopefully, this will help you to make a logical decision on whether or not the game is for you?

My only objective here is to educate you with the real and true facts that exist in the ghetto games. I'm not trying to inspire you to do wrong, nor do I encourage anyone to get involved in any type of criminal activities. I only desire to teach you the rules to the ghetto games, so that you can determine what is right or wrong for you! And make the decisions as to the path that you should choose to take. I took mine, and it resulted in almost a lifetime in the prison system. And many others have made the same bad decisions and mistakes that I've made. That's why now, you have something that we never had that will provide you with a better understanding of the game that a lot of us who fucked our life off didn't have, a chance ***not*** to make that same mistake as we did. We all only have one life to live, and the choices that you make will surely determine the outcome of your journey through life.

So in delivering this new and powerful urban message to you, it's only right that you pass this information along to your friends, comrades, family, brothers, and cousins! Because the more people who become aware of these very important rules, then the better the game would be, "No telling, this book might stop a young hustler from snitching on you, and others if he get's caught-up, or it might even save your life." The game is deep, and the more people who know about it, then the better off we all are. "Feel me!"

Also, feel free to log onto my website at www.Ghettotheory.com and post your comments and opinions of this new powerful urban lit.

Remember, don't hesitate to download my other E-Books entitled; "Ghetto Games, 1, 2 & 3, Natural Born Gangster, Double Trouble and Am I My Sister's Keeper! Also in paper back.

They are a must read, and I highly encourage every young male in the world to read a copy. Because it will change the way you live, understand, and perceive life.

Devoted to Lacing you!
G-prince

"Am I my brother's Keeper?"
January 16, 2013

Rule 1.

Silence and Secrecy!

One of the first rule that a young gangsta or hustler should know and fully follow, is to keep all criminal related acts and information about you and others strictly to yourself. There are so many hustlers in jails and in prisons all over the world, who made the mistake of telling their business to another person {friend associates, lovers, or family member} who in return, turned around and told the same information to the police or federal agents out of spite, or so they could benefit somehow. Usually, the other person got caught-up in a petty crime or major criminal case, and decided to use you as their escape-goat. You know, tell the police of your criminal acts so they could try to get a lesser sentence. And the next thing that you know, your ass is in jail wondering how you got caught up on a crime that you thought you got clean away on.

Let me share a short story with you. I know a young hustler who was coming up in the game doing bank robberies. Him and his crew would run into the bank and lay everyone down on the ground...'Just like the movie set it off." And one particular time, as they were running out of the bank from putting down a robbery, a police car just so happen to be close by and pulled up on the scene right when they were fleeing out from the bank, and instead of giving up, they turned their guns on the police car and open fire on the police as they ran away and jumped into a stolen car that was waiting for them.

They just happen to get away clean with over three hundred thousand dollars. After splitting the money three ways, they all left and went their separate ways. One of the robbers was so pumped up and excited about the robbery, that he went home and told his girlfriend that he live with all of the crazy details. She naturally shared in his excitement, and they had a lot of fun spending the money together.

His money, new cars, and his new look, brought him a lot more attention from the ladies and as you know "A ghetto dog will always stray, and play in the ghetto game". Until one day, his girlfriend came home early from work and found her scandalous girlfriend and her man caught up in the heat of passion.

Naturally a fight broke out, and before it was all over, the police was called by the neighbors and arrived on the scene. The friend got the worse end of the ass-whip-pen', so she despitefully mentioned that the affair between her and the other girls man, had been going on for a few months now, and that she was two months pregnant with his baby.

This news was like the ultimate disrespect to her girlfriend's emotions, and once she arrived at the police station to get booked on assault charges, she decided to get revenge on her boyfriend, so she told the police about the bank robbery that he and is friends committed.

And two hours later, her boyfriend and his crew was in Federal custody indicted on arm robbery charges and attempted murder on the police officer. Consequently, they all were found guilty and received a sixty-five year sentence in the Federal Pen.

There is an old saying that goes; "If the duck would have never quacked, then he would not have given up his position and ended up on the hunter's dinner table". In other words, if nobody knows your secrets, and you don't tell on yourself, you'll remain untouchable.

Truthfully, one of the biggest mistakes that a young hustler usually make is telling other people about his criminal acts or business.

If a person *isn't* involved with the situation, then it's none of their business. So, if you're the type of person that likes to brag, make-up jokes, or confide in people when you know you're doing or did something wrong, then you should never pretend to be a true hustler, and you should walk away from the game now and save yourself the misery of spending a lifetime in prison system.

Also, remember if you're playing the game, then you should know that if you are ever questioned by the police about anything, ***"then you have the right to remain silent,"*** and you should always exercise that right'. Because when you try to justify your where about, then those lies, or stories can get you twisted-up in way more trouble then if you had just kept your month shut, and requested an attorney.

Rule 2.

Do Your Dirt By Yourself!

This is another one of those rules that should really be considered if you chose to involve yourself in any type of criminal activities. Because the penitentiaries are packed full of people who trusted and relied on another criminal to do their dirt with. A lot of times we find our self to be a bad judge of character.

How many times have you trusted someone with a secret or relied on someone only to be deceived or disappointed in the end. Truthfully, you never know who you can really trust, until they are placed in a dangerous or threatening situation and they prove themselves loyal under pressure. And most of the time, you won't find out that your crimee is weak, until it's too late. Especially, considering that a lot of these so called gangsta's, hustlers, killers, and thugs, are playing the game by a different set of rules.

They do not respect the code of ethics that the game was originally laid down with, and therefore, the honor among the hustlers, thugs, and gangsta' has been terribly compromised. "Honor among thieves," not anymore!

Even so-called killers are getting caught up and snitching on other drug dealers and criminals so they can receive a lesser sentence. "Ain't that a bitch"! And in most cases, it's the ones that you never thought would do it.

Look at Frank Lucas, the kingpin drug dealer out of New York that they just did a movie about. A cold hustler, Killer, Kingpin, but in the end, he turned snitch to save his own ass. Who would've ever thought that a man with such a thorough ghetto resume' would violate the rules to the game and turn snitch in the end. So tell me, who can you really trust in the game?

It's true, betrayal hurts but it's a part of life that shouldn't be ignored. Crime done by yourself is considered the crime that's best done, because as I've mentioned before, if you don't tell on yourself, then you should be alright. And if you can't put the lick down yourself, then maybe you should think about getting into another line of work. Because the more people involved, the greater your chances are of getting caught. And don't think that just because you and your crew were successful in getting away and enjoying the benefits, that it can't catch-up with you in the future. Because you never know who might run their mouth to the wrong person and get you caught-up on some

Mickey Mouse shit. See the story in rule one; Silence and Secrecy.

So I ask you; "does crime really pay"? The prison system is filled with a lot of gangsta's, thugs, and hustlers, who would express to you the same thoughts. So make sure that every move that you make is properly planned and strongly calculated, because your very freedom depends on it.

Rule 3.

Never Pull a Gun and Not Use It.

One of the biggest mistakes that a person can make in life is pulling a gun on someone and not using it. Too many so call gangsta's has fell victim to this rule. Because they tend to underestimate their rivalries, or someone who they might feel is weak or a busta', and try to put down a scare tactic by drawing down on someone to try to punk them. They might even decide to rob the person as well, thinking that the other person is soft or a busta', and suppose to just except it like a punk until the script flip, and the so call busta' got the gun in his hand. And guess what? The so call busta' is going to shoot, because he's scared that if he don't, then next time the other dude catch him slippin', his ass will be out. So he's going to shoot the other dude out of fear and intimidation.

I had an old friend who's dead behind doing the same silly shit. He considered everyone a busta' and sucka' and use to run around and jack people for their drugs, jewelry, and money. Until one time he jacked this young hustler who was just coming up big in the game. He caught the young hustler slippin' in the parking lot of the club. And draw down on the young hustle and took his dope, money, and jewelry, and then slapped him in the head with the gun and told the young hustler to leave before he decide to put some hot rocks in his ass. Of course the young hustler ran off scared, embarrassed, and mad. Twenty minutes later, the young hustler crept-up on my friend with a twelve gage shot gun, and blow my friends whole face off.

"Yeah, an ugly sight, huh!" To pull a gun on someone for any reason is serious situation in everyway. If you're trying to protect yourself, possessions, or love ones from someone with scandalous intentions, then this is understandable. But, if your just trying to bluff your enemy or someone for silly or foolish reasons, then your destine to run into someone who's not going to except this kind of disrespect, and take your bluff personally. And it's no fun when your enemy got the gun. Also, to pull a gun on someone is a serious threat on that persons life, and no threat is suppose to be token lightly or ignored. So keep this in mind when you're out there playing those ghetto games.

Also, there's a flip side to this issue. Say Robert pulls a gun on Mike and threatens to kill him in front of a crowd of people, and then leave. Sam can also have a beef with Mike and decide to take advantage of this opportunity to get his revenge, and creep up and blast Mike when no one's around. And say that Mike dies, who do you think is going to get that murder beef? Yes, Robert! "Because all of them people who was around when Robert pulled his gun out on Mike, is now witnesses against Robert. And Robert's ass will need a dream team to ever have a chance at proving his innocence.

So be smart and remember never pull out your gun on a person and not use it. You'll be better off shooting him in the leg or shooting at him and missing, then to just walk away thinking that he's to scared to do anything about it. At least you know now, that you and he are enemies for life, and that you can never trust him again, "If you're smart!"

So now that you're in the game, then play by the rules. Don't be exposing your gun around people letting them know that you're strapped. That ain't no-bodies business but yours. If a person knows that you always be strapped, then they got the upper hand on you, because he knows that he got to come correct, or if he or she decide to try to set you up, then they know they have to get the drop on you. But, if they don't expect you to be strapped, then you got the element of surprise, and this can possibly be the upper hand that you need to save your life.

So keep your gun hidden at all times, and never pull it out if you don't plan on using it. *"This advice is given for protection purposes only*.......feel me!"

Rule 4.

Know The Consequences Of Everything That You Do!

A person should always know the laws in the state that they're doing there dirt in. Because it's some very simple laws that when broken, can carry very harsh penalties. A lot of hustlers don't take the time to educate them selves on this, and this is one of the main reason's why people are giving the game a black eye.

A lot of people just tend to jump into the game without knowing the rules or the real consequences that the crime will carry if they get caught-up. And the next thing you know, they mess around and get caught-up and can't take the pressure, because of the time that the crime carries, so they break bitch and start telling on everybody.

See, what a lot of you young hustlers don't know is, that there are a lot of crimes that you can get a life sentence for, or enough time that you will feel that the judge tried to give you close to a life sentence.

One law that every young urban male should be aware of is "Crack Cocaine." The reason is that Feds are giving out a 100 to 1 gram difference between a person who get's caught with crack cocaine compared to powder cocaine. "If this law ain't targeting the urban community then nothing is."

So basically, a young urban male can get caught with 50 grams of crack cocaine and get a ten years to life sentence, when you would have to be caught with 5000 grams of powder cocaine to get the same sentence in federal court. So, basically, if you sell cocaine cooked up in rock form, then they can wash your ass up with a lot of prison time. That's why a lot of young blacks are only selling powder cocaine now; they're getting hip to the game. And they never keep over 18 zones soft in one spot at a time, nor do they sell over 18 zones at one time.

However, there's a gang of laws that's targeted toward the urban areas, but if you don't know about them, then you will most likely fall victim to them. So it's always good to have an attorney that will keep you up dated and well informed on the new and current laws.

Other then this, what you need to really consider while you're out there paper chasing is, if you fall, then what do you stand to loose, and can you deal with it?

Here are some of the obvious consequences that you should strongly consider. "If you get busted, then you will have to go to prison for many years or for life!" Your wife or woman would most likely leave you while you're in prison....because, majority of them do! You will miss seeing your kids grow up, mature, and go through their little problems and complicated ordeals. Your family members will go through a lot of difficult times without your strength and support by their side, and some will possibly die while you're locked up. You can get sick and not receive the proper medical treatment that you need, and die while in prison. "No sex! Everybody that you thought was real and down for you, will eventually go on with their life and leave you for dead. And to make matters even worse, you will loose control over your life and have limited movement."

This is just a few realistic thoughts that has came to mind, but it's way more stressful then words can ever be express on paper.

Nevertheless, if you think that you can deal with all of the losses that I've mentioned herein, then the game is for you, but, if you cannot, then don't fool yourself and still play the game, because it ain't for you.

You'll know like everybody else knows, that sooner or later you're going to roll the dice and crap out, and if you can't handle the pressure or stand the consequences, then your going to end up doing like many other hustlers who has gotten themselves catch-up in something that is to much for them to handle, and end up selling their soul to the devil for a deal and a snitch jacket, and prison ain't no place for a snitch, so choose your path wisely and remember, the smart one, is the one who knows how to get out of the game and invest their winnings before they end up rolling the dice and crapping out on the game of life.

Choose your path carefully so that you understand the consequences of your actions.

Rule 5.

Always Follow Your First Mind.

One of the most powerful senses that a person has in the game of life is his instincts. Your six senses and intuition are nine times out of ten right. But, for some odd reason, we tend to ignore the vibes that we receive and do the opposite, which most of the time results in a bad situation. Think about it, how many times have you received that vibe that told your thoughts not to do something, or to not go somewhere, and you ignored it and went anyway, and ended up caught up in a bad situation.

Yeah, you feel where I'm coming from, but lets' consider that scenario on a more street level. Have you ever had a vibe that a person wasn't right around you? Like they were up to something or you just received a erry vibe around that person, and then you find out that he or she was rotten to the core! Maybe you received this vibe right before you went to serve someone and got busted or jacked. Or maybe, your girl told you to stay at home, and you ignored her and went out chasing that money, and then ended up in jail or something.

I can't really explain the true power of this gift that we have been given to perceive trouble or problems before hand, but I know that it's real and it's something that should never be ignored or taken lightly. I think that it's something that dogs and animals is more in tune with, but we have a more superior intellect, so our intelligence seems to supersede this unique sense that we find hard to master. But to learn how to recognize and master this special gift, will surely be a blessing to anyone in life as well as in the game. Because it's like a hidden alarm that let us know that something ain't right, or a problems and troubles is ahead.

Women are more in tune with this sense then men but, if you are conscious enough to tap into this special power, then I suggest that you do so, because this can truly save your life in the long run! "If your thoughts are telling you that somebody around you ain't right, then you better believe that you're not receiving those signals for nothing".

So learn how to master self, and believe in the powers that has been placed within you. Because, everything has been given to you for a reason, you just need to learn how to use it.

Rule 6.

Don't Let No Man Ever Punk You or Disrespect You!

Once you're caught up in the street game, then it's a must that you should always keep it gangsta' until you decide that it's time to get out. And one thing that you should never allow, and that's to let anyone punk you out, disrespect you, or to take anything from you. Because if you ever let someone get away with disrespecting you or taking something from you, then news will travel like that internet and everyone will think that they can get away with doing it also.

I was always raised and molded to always be a strong man and never allow another person to get over on me or punk me, so whenever another man decided that he wants to disrespect me or violate my space, then we're going to fight... win, lose or draw. We're going to fight! Whatever don't kill you, will only make you stronger, and in the game you can't afford to let other people believe that they can get away with disrespecting you, or to get over on you. It's the laws of the street game, either you live by it or fall victim to it.

There's no other way to play it!

Now don't get the game confused. Some issues will call for more extreme measures, so don't think that a fist fight will resolve all situations, because in the street game, you got to know when to fight and when to take it to the next level.

Respect is something that you must earn and demand, as well as give in those scandalous streets, and this goes to say, "If you don't stand for something, then you will most likely fall for anything."

Also, if you're in prison then this rule must really apply, because if you show any type of weakness, then other prisoners will most likely try to prey on you, but if they see that you're not going to tolerate shit then, they will back up off you. You must always remember that the next man bleeds like you, and can be hurt like you, so fear no man. Even if you do loose the first fight, then the ass woopen' that you receive would just make you fight better and harder the next time. And also, make your fight game better. If you punk out and allow another man to disrespect you purposely, then you might as well be his bitch, because everyone who see it, will loose respect for you and also try to take advantage of you. And if they see that you're really a punk, then someone will end up turning you out and have you wearing kool-aid on your lips and walking with a sick

24

sway in your hips. So never be scare to fight someone who intentionally disrespects you, a lot of times you will see that a lot of nigga's really can't fight at all.

Listen, even when you run into that fool who tries to disrespect you because he got the numbers on his side then, try to play it cool and just walk away. And as soon as you catch him by his self, then beat the shit out of him! Sometimes you got to walk away when you're out numbered, but when the situation is in you're favor, then show him how a real gansta' gets down.

Also, sometime you can't walk away when you're out numbered, but it's always away to win, as long as you got the heart to go hard. A lot of fools will start running when the blood start to fly, so don't never count your loses until it's over. Until then, keep it gansta' and never except no disrespect from no one!

Rule 7.

Never Give Out More Then You Can Stand to Lose

This is a very important rule because it can be the difference between you falling off or staying afloat. Therefore, you should never give somebody something on consignment that can break you or put you in a fucked up situation or in debt.

See, when you give out shit on consignment anything can happen, that person can get caught up, robbed, or get a set of nuts and decide to say fuck you and try to run off.

Now if you accept it, then everyone will try you. If you catch up with him and put some hot rocks in him, now you take a chance on him telling on you and getting you caught up on that. So, to save yourself some unnecessary problems, don't give a person enough to hurt you if you have to take that kind of lost.

Also, something small won't seduce a person thoughts to do something crazy like run off, because it's more beneficial to them if they keep it real with you, knowing that the little work that your providing them is keeping them afloat. And they know that they can rely on you to be there for them, when they finally get finish with the last work that you gave them.

Also, understand that by doing this, you're basically relying on someone else's hustle. So you're putting your fate and profit in someone else's hands, hoping that they are reliable and thorough. Even a bank won't give certain people a loan if their credibility and credentials isn't right. So you should try to use this same standard in considering the people that you decide to trust. Because a lot of people are more problems then profit. And remember if you chose to trust a person who uses, then eventually you would end up taking a lost, so understand a hustler's down fall is always his trust and bad judgment. And his gain is always the profit that he secures and properly invests for hard times.

Rule 8.

Never Work For Another Hustler

To me, that front shit is punk shit! And this is something that I don't suggest anyone should fuck with. But, let's not get the game twisted, because a lot of nigga's like being another hustler's flunky, and the game is set up so everyone is suppose to play there position. So if you're a pawn, solder, or flunky, then play your position to the fullest. But the way that I see it, why would I want to take high risk and get low income pay? If the only way that you can get on is by consignment, then after flipping one or two sacks then it's time to buy your own work and grind for yourself. No man really respects another hustler who's depending on him to eat or provide for him and his family needs. So as a small hustler, you'll only be used and abused in the game.

And remember if the Feds come into the picture and crack the big man, then guess what? You can get placed into the big conspiracy and even though you were just a little fish making crumbs, you can still get big fish time. As long as they can connect you as one of his workers or someone that he constantly dealt with, then you can get the same time as him. Even if you didn't know how much work he was moving. So if your taking a chance of getting big fish time, then you might as well do big fish grind.

Listen, the prisons is filled with little fishes that ended up in a big conspiracy and got a life sentence behind being the big fish flunky or runner. Can you imagine how stupid that fool feels every morning that he wake up, knowing that he fucked his life off for just a couple of chicken shit zones, or a couple of G's. He was basically getting pimped by the big fish, and when it was all over, he didn't end up with nothing but a gang of time to think about his foolish mistakes. There's a gang of people who position in life is a flunky's so if that's your position, then play your part. But, if you're a true hustler, then hustle for your self, and be accountable for your own mistakes, problems, and actions. If I'm gambling for high stakes, then I want big bank!

Also, understand when you work for another hustler, no matter how or why you come up short, you still own the debt. And now you really work for the big fish until his money is paid back, and in this game, your soul is your collateral, so don't play yourself short, stand on your own two feet, and if you can't make money, then get the fuck out of the way and get you a damn nine to five, before you get yourself killed. Because the game is not to be taken for a joke!

Rule 9.

Don't Never Let Your Face Show You're True Emotions or Intentions When You're Mad.

You should never let another man or woman be able to read your thoughts or true intentions when you're pissed off. And one of the main things that you should learn how to master the control of, your facial expressions and body language, because this can be a dead give away. A lot of people who don't know how to control these assets will be the type who you will see that will always get loud and crazy as they throw their little temper tantrums. This can be considered a big weakness, because you allow other people the opportunity to read your thoughts, and they can use this to deceive you in the long run. Because, they learn how you act and react toward certain situations, so if they were trying to deceive you, then they will know if you really believe them because your actions will tell on your thoughts.

Also, if you're mad at a person then you automatically put them on point, and if they believed that you would or could become a treat to them, then they got the opportunity to act first, because you have a bad habit of telegraphing your emotions and thought.

A real master of the game can be around their worse enemy, someone who they want to punish, and nobody in the crowded room would ever know. He would smile and play it all the way off, and the person who he is plotting on will never know.

Similar to you running into a beautiful and sexy lady that you started kicking it with on the down low, and then later on our homeboy throw a big party and the same beautiful and sexy lady that you've been creeping on the down low with, shows up to the party with her husband who is your homeboy friend from work. Of course, you and her are surprised, but no one at the party would ever know that you and your homeboy's friend's wife are lovers, but you two! You would play it off like she doesn't even exist in the room. You might even flirt with a couple of other ladies around her just to add to your little secret game, but all and all, the truth would remain a secret from everyone.

This is the same way that you should learn how to hide and camouflage your thoughts, feelings, and true intentions from others, especially if you're mad or harboring hatred for someone. Because, the less that someone can read your thoughts, then the better that your position becomes. They get relaxed around you and put their guards down, so when you decide to come for that ass, then they will be totally surprised and shocked.

The element of surprise is 95% percent effective so learn how to hide your emotions and if possible, place the thoughts in a person mind that you want them to have. But always know why you want them to have these particular thoughts.

Have a purpose and reason for your actions and you will become the master of your game.

This goes for your woman too! Learn her emotions, feeling, facial expressions, and body language, but learn how to keep her off balance by yours. Basically, you must do things to throw her thoughts off here and there, and make false emotional acts like temper tantrum within her presence, to see how she reacts to it. If she does something silly that you don't like and you throw a fake temper tantrum at her, either she's going to check herself next time when she does it, or she'll do it on purpose to see if she can piss you off again. If she does, then you know that she has a mind full of deception, and that's a bad sign.

If she isn't 100% percent in your corner, about you, and for you, then she's against you! *"It is-what it is"*.

Your actions and reactions means a lot in life, especially when your caught up in the game, so master your emotions and expressions and make them become the tools that you use to control your surroundings.

Rule 10.

Don't Never Shit Where You Eat and Lay You're Head at!

This concept is another rule that should be engraved in stone. But, the crazy thing is to many hustlers don't live by this rule and they always find out the hard way that when you do your dirt the same place that you lay your head at, then your like a sitting duck just waiting for the hunter to come along and catch you slipping.

First of all, you should never keep your work and money in the same spot, because if you loose one then you loose them both.

Secondly, you should never keep work where you lay your head at, or sell your work out of the same spot that you lay your head at. And I say this because; it's like broad casting your business to the police. If you're doing illegal activities, then it suppose to be done with some sort of secrecy and discreetness. Or your ass won't last long at all.

Thirdly, if you're in the game, then no one is suppose to know where you're laying your head at. A lot of you fools like to plush out your secret spot where you lay your head at, and then use the same spot as a place where you take them pretty big butt ladies at, to show off your pimped out taste, and to get your little freak on.

But little do you know, those same pretty "big butt" ladies are with other players who are paying them "big butt" ladies money, or a percentage of the lick, to put them up on the places where other hustlers in the game reside at. And next thing that you know, your ass will be laying faced down on your living room floor in handcuffs, while niggas in ski mask is pointing guns to your head and threatening to kill you for your work and money.

Believe me, many good hustlers has fell victim to the "big butt" and a smile scenario. And you don't know what woman, got a friend or a brother, or maybe a boyfriend that's on that kind of time. The lady that you might meet and take to your spot might be a total square, or not that type of scandalous lady, but one day she might drop by with her girlfriend or even drive by your secret spot with her girlfriend, and casually mention that you stay at a certain condo complex, and that could be enough to get you set up in the game. So as long as your in the game hustling, then keep your spot secret to just a very selective and chosen few family members. And make sure that you let them know that you don't want them to bring people over to your house, or tell people where you live at. And take them pretty "big butty" women to the dame motel! "That's what the motel is for, one night freak sessions." Your secret spot is for your privacy and safety, and should be respected in this way.

I know that when you're out there in the game you tend to take things for granted, but you got to remember that the game is serious. And scandalous niggas' and bitches would set you up and kill you for them crumbs.

The street game is full of deception and manipulation, and if you don't take the game serious, then it would eat your dumb ass up alive. You'll either be dead or imprison... or both! You got to be on top of your game at all times, and conscious of your surroundings. If your working and laying your head at the same place, then either your not really having no money and you need to go find you a good nine to five before you fuck around and loose your life over some crumbs. Or if your kind of light weight ballin', then your a fool and won't last to much longer. Because either the jackers is coming to get you or the police, there is no other way to perceive this. Maybe, you had a little good run, but if you don't know how to put up a better security system for you and your love ones, then when you fall, you can bet that you will loose it all, because the police is taking everything that they think that you purchased with that money. And it's obvious, your not to hard to find. In other works, be smart and do your best to secure yourself, or realize that you're just in the way. And save yourself some unnecessary pain and problems, and get the hell out of the game while you're somewhat ahead in your profit and gains. Because, nobody can last forever, and when nigga's get hit, then sometimes it's for good. So try not to be a statistic.

Rule 11.

Never Go to War Over a Bitch.

The impotency of this rule should never be ignored or taken lightly. Because there is a whole lot of niggas' laying in the grave yard and walking the penitentiary yard, because they were sprung dumb and pussy whooped on a woman who wasn't devoted to them. A lot of niggas try to put claims on a woman like you own her, but the crazy thing is, that you're the only one that believes that she's yours. She might just enjoy having sex with you. As well as all the other hustlers that you don't know about, but instead of you just enjoying the moment, you want to try to put some type of claims or locks on a woman who's a cold freak. "You got to be one of the dumbest fools in the world!"

Peep, let me try to give you some real game! If another man takes your lady, then she wasn't really your in the first place, and I don't care if you were married with kids by her, she still wasn't yours mentally or emotionally. So you should not under any circumstances, go and confront another man about the scandalous shit that your bitch has done. If she goes out and have sex with another man, then you can't do nothing but either except it, or shake her ass! But, to go and confront another man about him fucking your so call lady is some serious sucka shit. "Truthfully, if you think that your lady is fuckin another nigga, then nine times out of ten, you're probably right.

"It is-what it is."

Now the only way that you should confront another nigga about your lady, is if you know that she's totally down and devoted to you, and another nigga jumped out there and disrespect her or put his hands on her. Then you should put your foot deep in his ass, because when you got a women that's 1000% percent down and devoted to you, then she's a reflection of you, and when someone disrespect her, then they disrespect you to. And I'm not talking about a bitch that you're just fucking. "I'm talking about a woman who's living with you and is totally about you." Not just a woman that you're dating. Because you don't know what a women that your just fucking or dating is doing when she's not with you, and she might try to get you to jump out there with another one of her lovers who probably dogged her, and you not knowing what your getting caught-up in, because you can confront him, and he can get highly offended about you approaching him like a sucka and about his bitch, and put some hot rocks in your ass. Now your dead and he's in prison while she's out still fuckin who she wants.

How would you feel being in prison with a life sentence over killing another nigga that your bitch was fucking on the side? Do you think that she's going to be there for you while you're in prison with a life sentence? "You know damn well she isn't!"

As soon as your dumb and crazy ass get locked up, then she's going to be out at the club wearing that sexy red low cut dress that all the niggas like. I know that you think that I'm over exaggeration! But I can assure you, that there is a gang of niggas who fell victim to this same type of situation.

A real nigga is going to just laugh at the bitch and roll out like a player if he find-out that she's fucking another man. Because a man now-a-days, got about ten to one odd on women in our society. Basically because, there's so many men who's lock up in the prison system. So to fight over a woman who chooses to be a freak, is a sucka characteristic! I don't care if you walk into your house early from work, and catch your wife, baby mamma, or lady in the bed with another man. It's not his fault at all, because your woman is foul for disrespecting you like this, not him...he's just being a dog ass nigga' that he is. So, to

41

try to jump on him isn't right, because it's your bitch that has disrespected you. So basically, your thoughts should be address toward her, and a true player would just tell her to pack her shit-up and get the fuck out.

"Of course, you're going to be pissed and probably want to kick some ass". But really, you're winning by being able to kick your problems to the curb. And if you put your hands on her, or on him, then it would just flip the script and put you in a fucked up position if and when, the police shows up.

Remember regardless of the freaky circumstances, you violated the law by assaulting them and your ass is going to jail. So play it smart and keep your game tight. "A scandalous bitch is just a scandalous bitch, and there is no other way to look at her."

A woman should always have the freedom to choose who she want to be with, or be down with, so if she chooses some one other then you, then keep it real and move on. There's plenty of real and beautiful woman out there who's looking for a good and *Real Man*. So when one falls astray, then remember there's always two or three more that will be happy to take her place.

Rule 12.

Always Save For a Rainy Day.

I cannot begin to tell you how many so called "ballers" is in prison dead broke, because they fail to save for a rainy day. It's crazy, but you never know when you're going to fall off, and if you're not smart enough to plan and save for it, then you might really regret it in the future. The game is very unpredictable! You could easily take a big loss at any time, or catch a case and need bail money so you can get ghost, or money to retain a good attorney, or to be able to re-up! If you get popped and ain't got any money stashed, then your ass is out! "Especially if you get hit for everything."

A lot of hustlers in the game is only living for the moment, but they don't realize that the moment can come to an end at any time. So to think that all of those fly cars and jewelry can easily get confiscated in a police raid. And also, that safe at your mother's house might also get hit with a search warrant. So if you're not smart enough to put some of that money in the ground, or a safe in a secret spot that only you know, then you might experience a very disappointing lose.

Think about it, say that you do get popped and can afford to get you a pretty good attorney for say forty or fifty thousand dollars, and he gets you off with a good deal for say a ten year sentence. Yes, this is considered a real good deal in most cases! However, who will take care of your family while you are gone? Say that you were even fortunate enough to salvage another $25 g's, how long do you think that this will last you? Between taking care of your family and your first three to five years in prison, your ass will most likely be dead broke and mad as hell. Basically, because you were making all of that money and didn't do shit with it, but fuck it off on cars, clothes, jewelry, and trickin......! "Now you feel like a damn fool." Believe me, I know a gang of big time ballers' who was making and having millions in the game, but sitting in prison right now flat broke.

Look at the previews of American Gangsta's, the facts don't lie, and those ex-hustlers are considered the government trophies of all of the baddest and rawest hustlers that they took down and left them dead, in prison for life, or living life scared to death broke, with a snitch jacket on them. "A wise man not only learns from his own mistakes, but also from the mistakes of others!"

Listen hustlers, the one who benefits the most in the game is the one who puts forty or fifty thousand dollars in a small business that might bring them around twenty or thirty thousand dollars a year.

They might hypothetically, start a corporation in a different name and make it a small business investment cooperation or something, and have there yearly profits forwarded straight into their corporate bank account. This way nobody knows about it and they keep all of their documents in a private place like a safe deposit box.

So now when they are doing those ten years in prison, they know that when they get out, then they will have a pretty nice bit of paper stashed away. They become silent investors in things like beauty salons, clothing stores, clubs, and fast food restaurants. All of there investments is secret and done through their corporation, so as long as the taxes is paid on the profit, then they're cool.

Some hustlers have three to four investments like this and they're making about $100 to a 150g's a year. So they know that they will be cool when they get back out.

See, it may not seem like shit when you're out hustling and using the extra money to further your hustle. But in the end, it can make the difference between being broke or comfortable when it's all over. If a person thinks that they can play the game without taking a lost or falling, then he's a fool!

"Also, this book does not encourage any type of criminal activity, but, just uses fiction of real life illustration to try to encourage the younger generation to be smart, and know that there are criminal consequences toward breaking the law. So learn the rules of life.

"Do what's right and always strive to master the game!"

Rule 13

Always Plan out Your Moves and Don't Ever do Shit Without Carefully Thinking it over.

When you're caught up in the street game, that spare of the moment shit will get you caught up. You might get away with certain moves that you put down once or twice. But if you continue to jump out there on impulse, then sooner or later your ass is going to come up short, and the price to pay off stupid mistakes is usually the penitentiary yard or grave yard. So it's always good to be patient and properly plan out even the littlest situation, and that way, your chance of success will be even that much more possible.

When I was growing up in the game, I had an older homeboy who was a vicious stick up hustler. He basically specialized in jackin' drug dealers and other hustlers in the game. He would catch a nigga at the club drunk and slippin, and draw down on the nigga and his bitch....if she's present, and rob them for their money and jewelry. He might come up with $3 to $8 g's and around twenty to forty thousand dollars worth of jewelry. Also, he'll get the word on where another hustler lived at and catch the hustler coming home late at night drunk, and draw down on the hustler handcuff him and walk him into his spot and rob him for his money, dope, and jewelry. My homeboy was good at what he did, and his little ghetto wealth kind of complimented his success.

But, as time progressed, he got arrogant and started slippin in his normal ways in planning and strategizing his moves. He stumbled across a nigga who was considered a Baller in the game, and seen the nigga get out of his bucket with a big duffle bag and he know that it was either filled with money or dope, so he grabbled his gun and jumped out of his car in quick pursuit of the nigga with the duffle bag. They were at a motel and it was around eleven o'clock at night, so the motel was quit yet kind of full.

The Baller with the duffle bag went into the motel room where he was headed and my homeboy creped up on the side of the Baller's car and waited for him to come out, and when the Baller finally came out and walked over to his car, my homeboy jumped out with his gun drown. The Baller was surprise and went for his gun, and my homeboy gunned him down, then went over and grabbed the duffle bag from around the Baller's arm, and when he raised back up, he saw the police running from every where and they had him dead caught.

My homeboy knew that he was caught slippin because he was surrounded by police with guns drown, and a dead body at his feet. So he decided to go out like a gangster and raised his gun at the police and started unloading it as they lite his ass up from all directions. Just that quick his game came to a crazy and deadly end. See, the Baller was being set up on a drug deal with some undercover police, and my homeboy stumbled into the situation blindly, not realizing that the police was posted all around him. He jumped out there on some spontaneous shit, and it cost him his life, just that quick!

If he would have taken his time and analyzed the situation, then he probably would have seen the trap and not fell victim to it. All money ain't good money in the game, and if you don't plan to succeed, then it's obvious that you plan to loose.

Also remember, anger can cloud your better judgment and cause you to make irrational decisions. So it's always good to wait until you're better focus and have properly thought the problems out, before making a decision to do something while you're mad or caught up in your emotions. At times certain situations isn't as bad as it may seem, and if they are, then to properly think them out can only help you deal with them better, and in the right way. So try not to do things spontaneously or while you're deeply involved and caught up in your feeling, "Because making the wrong choice and mistake in life can cost you dearly."

Rule 14.

A Good Woman is Always a reflection of Her Man!

If you're caught up in the game and you got that special lady in your life that you consider your number one, then it's essential that you should thoroughly lace her in the things that she needs to know to be able to deal with certain complex situations. Her knowledge of the street game can be the determining factor of your success or down fall.

Let me explain. The first thing that a jacker wants to know is where you live at. If they catch your lady in traffic in her new escalade truck, the first thing that they're going to try to do is follow her ass home. So, if she's not sharp enough to notice a tail, then she can lead the haters straight to your main spot. And next thing you know, niggas will be in your house with ski mask on threatening to kill you and her for your stash.

Also, a lot of women is running around town and bragging to their girlfriends about your business. "When you go out of town, when you're out taking care of your business, and about all of the nice things you do for her." So your lady's so-called girlfriend is probably harboring a lot of hidden jealous emotions. So if your lady starts telling her girlfriend's to much of your business, then her

51

girlfriend's might be secretly telling this some information to her broke ass boyfriend, who in exchange, might be plotting to put a lick down on you. He might not come on the lick himself, but instead, send his little cousins on the lick at you. And this can get you and your girl fuck off.

Also, niggas try to start rumors about you fucking and getting other women pregnant, so they can make your lady mad at you and if she's young and naive, then she will become venerable to another man's seduction, and if another nigga is able to get your lady to lay and play, then he can also get her to cross you up. "Similar to hacking into your computer and plants a virus, once a person infiltrate your foundation, then he has access to all of your data and wealth."

As you can tell, the game is way deeper then the average hustler can perceive. And although you might have your game tight, you still must take the initiative to make sure that your wife, baby's momma, or main lady's game is tight as well. You see, when you're caught up in the street game, you never know when you might get busted, jacked, or have to punish a nigga for getting out of line. Ask yourself? Can your lady deal with the psychological mind games of the police, if they snatch her up and try to question her about your activities?

Of course, the less that she knows about your illegal dealings, the better off you both are, and you should never put her deep off into your business, but instead, just let her play her part, and school her on how to deal with certain situations such as police raid or if you get busted. She should know who your attorney and your bail-bond men are. Also, if you got to serve some time, she should know what you expect of her. The better you lace your main lady, the better off you will be, because her position in life is your soulmate, and if no one else, you better be able to trust her, because if not, then you'll never survive the real struggles of the game. "Believe me!"

Rule 15.

Choose Your Friends and Comrade Wisely

"Lord, please protect me from my friends, for I can handle my enemies!" It's a true fact that the close ones to you are always the ones who poses the biggest threat. And this is simply because when you're caught up in the ghetto games, you're constantly watching out for all of the potential enemies that you feel and believe could pose a serious threat to you. But the friends and comrades that you accept in your life is given a lot of unnoticed lead way, which could easily result in a big problem if they ever decided to betray your trust.

It's so many occasions when a close friend or comrade decides to turn the table or flip the script on their best friend over some money, dope, or a bitch. The game got a lot of scandalous thoughts. You got a lot of niggas who got jealous of their main-man because of his ghetto rich status, and end up jacking and killing him when then felt that they had the opportunity to get away with it.

Other situations can trace back to niggas who use to go and rob and jack together and when they stumble across a big lick, one of the jackers get greedy and decide to kill his partner and take all of the money and dope for him self.

Then you got the nigga who's a sucka for a bad bitch, and after the woman getting him sprung on the sex, the woman start putting them scandalous thoughts in his mind to make him jealous of his homeboy's wealth or position in the game, and eventually conveniences the sucka to rob or jack his comrade, so they can have more for themselves or so the sucka can become the big man instead of the little man.

See a lot of us would never think that our comrades would ever cross us out like this, but just the same, you got a lot niggas who never thought their closes comrade or blood brother would end up snitching on them. But it happens!

However, the question is what can we do to prevent or protect our selves from getting cross like this, and from what I've seen and analyzed in the game. There are a few methods that could be used to better become aware of some of these scandalous characters that tend to hide in some of our closes friends. Because it's a true fact that we always tend to see and notice a lot of signs and fucked up ways within our closes friends and comrades, but for some reason we choose to ignore them. And then when we end up getting cross up by them, then we always say that we knew it! "That is, if we are fortunate to live through it."

Now peep, one of the most common characteristic is jealousy. If you notice your comrade displaying little jealous ways, when he see the way people treat you or how women act toward you or when you're flossing a new car, lady friend, or jewelry, then you need to take heed to these feelings especially if your ballin way harder then him. I don't care if you're blessing the nigga with work trying to bring him up in the game with you.

"He got that Cain and Abel disease", and no matter how much you bring him up, he will still envy you." It's embedded in his character and sooner or later it will be exposed, and it might not turn out to well for you when it does. So do yourself a favor, and shake this scandalous nigga before he cross you. I don't care if you were raised with this sucka', or if he's your brother and will kill for you. He's infected, and this alone will become your biggest threat if you don't get rid of him from your life.

Another character flaw that you should look out for is when you get a comrade who's a sucka' for a bitch. You know the type. The one who always seems to fall in love or get sprung on the pussy! He can be a cold gangsta' in the streets, and a vicious rider when it comes to pushing that pistol, but if a bitch can break him down like a sucka', then nine times out of ten, she can also control his actions and thoughts. And if he runs across the right one, then your ass might end up face down in a puddle of blood with your safe open and empty. When pussy can control a persons emotions like that, then he could never be trusted, because he'll kill you over that bitch, so never trust a nigga with them type of sucka character flaws, because if he gets busted and is facing a lot of time, then no telling what he might do to not leave that pussy out there alone.

It's a fact that a true friend and comrade is priceless, and if you got one, two or a few on your team, then always keep it real with one another and take the time to lace each other up on the do's and don'ts of the rules to the street game.

As long as you and your comrades are playing by the same set of rules, then you're cool, but if you ain't, then you better shake them out of your game, because your foolish decision by not doing so, will cost you your life in the long run.

Rule 16.

Don't do the Crime if you Can't Do the Time

Listen, if your out there hustling in the street game, then there's a penalty to every crime that you choose to commit. Some are more harsher then others, but all and all, if your out their taking a chance with committing these crimes, then you need to be able to accept the punishment if you do end up getting caught-up. A lot of you so call hustlers, is getting cracked and getting scared like a busta', and turning snitch to try to get a lesser sentence. The police is pimping a lot of you so-called gangsta's like a bunch of hoes, because they're making you tell on other hustlers in the game, then given you a snitch jacket and throwing your sorry ass back to the wolves. Can you imagine being around a gang of real gangsta's who got told on by a snitch, and then they find out that you're a rat? Yeah, an ugly sight huh?

That little extra time that you got off for snitching ain't nothing compared to the hurt, pain, and unnecessary scares that you would suffer! And a lot of people who told won't make it out of the prison system alive. And don't think that no one is going to know about you, because the prison system is like the internet, word travels fast, and our paperwork would get checked at the door, so it's really impossible to get away with snitching.

For all you criminals who don't know. A lot of times you can get busted for a crime, but the evidence against you is so weak, that if you and your crimes keep your mouth shut, then eventually you would get your case dismissed and thrown out. But, before it get to that faze, the police usually separate you and your crimees and threaten all of ya'll, and make it seem like the other one broke weak just to scare you, and the next thing you know, all you guys start telling like bustas', and with that, they got all of the evidence that they need to give you'll more time then even they anticipated on giving you.

I know that it sounds crazy, but it never fails, if one out of four of you fall weak, then his statements will get you all washed up. But if you all keep your mouth shut, then the evidence has no real substance to stand on. Unless you all get busted dead bang, then you might as well just all wait for a good deal together. But, other then this situation, you must understand that the snitches are the ones who make up 90% percent of the convictions in the state and federal systems.

If you so called criminals start keeping your damn mouth shut, then you will have a 90% percent chance of beating the case against you. But, you got to keep it 100% percent real, and not let the government's head games scare you into deceiving yourself. They don't give a damn about you, your considered a piece of shit to them, so if you think that you got anything good coming from selling your soul to the devil, then kiss your ass good-bye, because if you don't respect the game, then the game will not have no respect for you, and prison is about respect, so your ass will have to pay the penalty one way or another. And that's as real as it gonna get!

Also, always remember this, the less people that you have with you when you commit a crime, then the better off you are, and the less people that know about your business, then the less chance that you have for a person to tell on you.

Learn to keep your mouth shut, and how to do your dirt by yourself. That way, if you get busted, then that means that your dumb ass told on yourself by telling someone else about your business. You probably bragged to one of your scandalous friends or jealous comrades who in return, told someone else who told the wrong person. Or you probably told your lady, and she got mad and pissed-off at you one day, and decided to get even with you by crossing you up. Believe me, you never know, nor can you ever predict the scandalous possibilities that come with deception, so learn how to keep your dirt to yourself so you won't have to worry about another person being able to tell on you.

Listen, the game is played by some strict and significant rules that are engraved in stone. So if you cannot honor these rules, then the game ain't for you.

When you violate these rules, you not only jeopardize your life, but also, the life of your love ones and those close to you. Because when you become a snitch, then you receive a death wish on you for a lifetime, and in some cases, if a person can't get to you, then they might try to take it out on your love ones.

Understand the penalties that you're face with in life if you choose to commit a crime then, be man enough to accept your punishment. If you can't do this, then get the hell out of the game, because that lifestyle isn't for you.

Ask yourself, can you do the rest of your life in prison? If your answer is no, then know that it's time to walk away from that criminal lifestyle. It's never hard to walk away when you know that you got your whole life ahead of you. You just got to be smarter then all of the other fools who thought that they could hustle for a lifetime.

All you have to do is go invest a couple of years in something productive like Real Estate or business, and then you can use your hustler wits in another aspect of the game. It beats spending lonely decades in the penitentiary wishing that you did. "So keep it real with your self and don't do the crime, if you're not willing to do the time."

Conclusion

In bringing this powerful urban literature to an end, I will like to leave you with some profound thoughts that I hope that you will live by and always cherish.

1. Always know the potential problems and consequences to every aspect of your thought, behavior, and action.

2. Trust is your greatest weakness in the street game.

3. To become successful, you must retire yourself from the game before getting killed in it, or before receiving an extreme prison sentence.

4. You must always strive to secure your money in some profitable business investments, so you can always be able to enjoy the benefits of your struggles.

5. Understand and honor the rules to the game.

6. Always strive to be wise in your choices and decision, because one mistake can hurt you. And always learn to study the thought, ways, and actions of the people whose apart of your struggle.

7. And if you can't live by the rules if you get caught and have to do the time, then leave it alone, because it's not for you.

G. Prince

Devoted to lacing you!

LOOK FOR *G. PRINCE* LATEST NEW
RELEASES IN BOOK STORES AND FOR
PURCHASE ON
www.ghettotheory.com
AMAZON.COM

FOR ADDITIONAL COPIES OF
RULES OF THE STREET GAME GO TO:

GHETTO THEORY PUBLISHING

Presents

Ghetto Games

Ghetto Games II, "the saga continues."

Am I My Sister's Keeper?

Natural Born gangster

**Rules of the Street Game that Every Hustler
Should Know...!**

Look for *"Ghetto Games III"*
coming soon March 2014

Ghetto Games 1 & 2,
they are the hottest urban faction tales written and a
must read for anyone who enjoys the mind twisting
drama of the ghetto street life and passion that feed our
ambitions to struggle against all odds.

DOUBLE TROUBLE

SMILE NOW.... DIE LATER

G. PRINCE
GHETTO THEORY PUBLISHING

This book is rated triple X for the extreme violent contents that has been realistically conveyed through the un-censorships that reflect the true urban struggles, and realities of the ghetto games.

Money, sex, murder, betrayal, drugs, and revenge only spells one thing, "Natural Born Gangster"

www.ingramcontent.com/pod-product-compliance
Lightning Source LLC
Chambersburg PA
CBHW071207130626
46555CB00004B/1615